This Little Hippo
book belongs to

_____

_____

For Rebecca

Scholastic Children's Books
Commonwealth House, 1-19 New Oxford Street
London WC1A 1NU, UK
A division of Scholastic Ltd

London ~ New York ~ Toronto ~ Sydney ~ Auckland
Mexico City ~ New Delhi ~ Hong Kong

First published in the UK in 1986 by André Deutsch Ltd
This edition published in 1997 by Little Hippo, an imprint of Scholastic Ltd

Text copyright © Brenda Smith, 1986
Illustrations copyright © Klaas Verplancke, 1997

ISBN 0 590 19805 X

Printed in Italy by Amadeus

6 8 10 9 7

The right of Brenda Smith and Klaas Verplancke to be identified
as the author and illustrator of this work have been asserted by them
in accordance with the Copyright, Designs and Patents Act, 1988.

Wake up, Charlie Dragon!

by
Brenda Smith

Illustrated by
Klaas Verplancke

Little Hippo

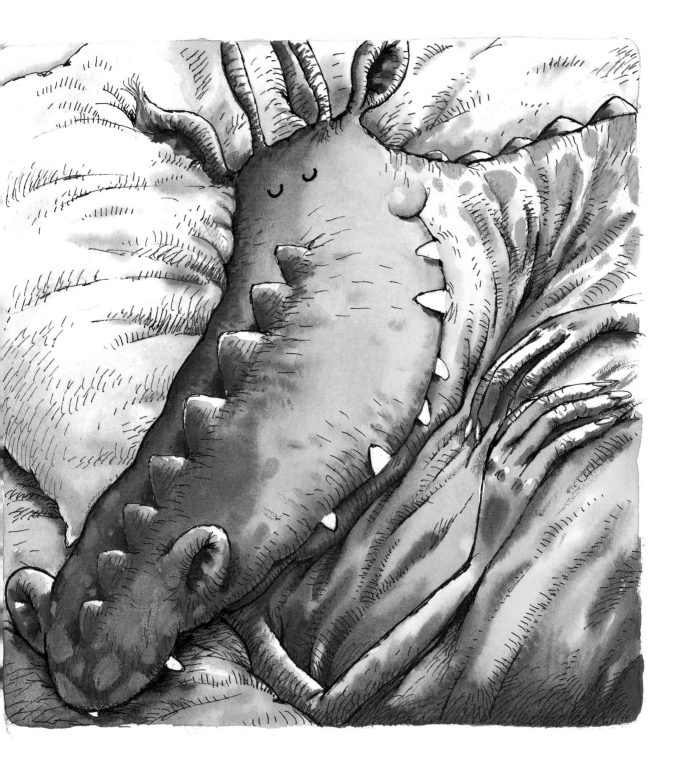

Charlie Dragon was asleep.

He had been asleep for almost a year.

He slept through Christmas . . .

He missed his presents.

He slept through Easter . . .

He missed his eggs.

He slept through Summer . . .

He missed all the fun.

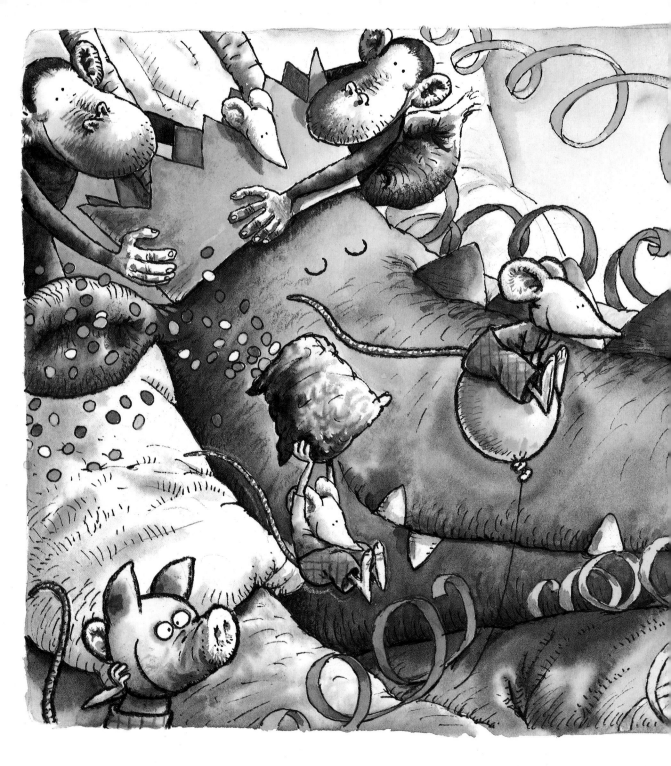

He slept through his birthday . . .

He missed the party.

He slept through Autumn . . .

He missed Hallowe'en.

Then one day . . . all the monkeys came down from
the trees; all the birds flew down from the sky;
strange creatures crawled out of the lake;

all the animals came out of the jungle.
And they all got together to shout:
"Wake up Charlie Dragon! We need you."

"Look Charlie Dragon – we're having a party."

"We need you to light our bonfire. Please wake up."

"Thank you Charlie Dragon!"

While all the animals enjoyed the bonfire party,
Charlie Dragon opened his Christmas presents.
He ate all his Easter eggs.

He opened all his birthday presents.

And then the monkeys brought out
Charlie's birthday cake and shouted,

"We're ready Charlie – would you
light the candles please?"

Charlie took a deep breath and then blew flames
across the top of the cake to light the candles.

Well done Charlie! All the animals joined in to sing,
"Happy Birthday to you, Charlie Dragon."

And then, after he had eaten
three slices of birthday cake,

Charlie Dragon went slowly
. . . back . . . to . . .

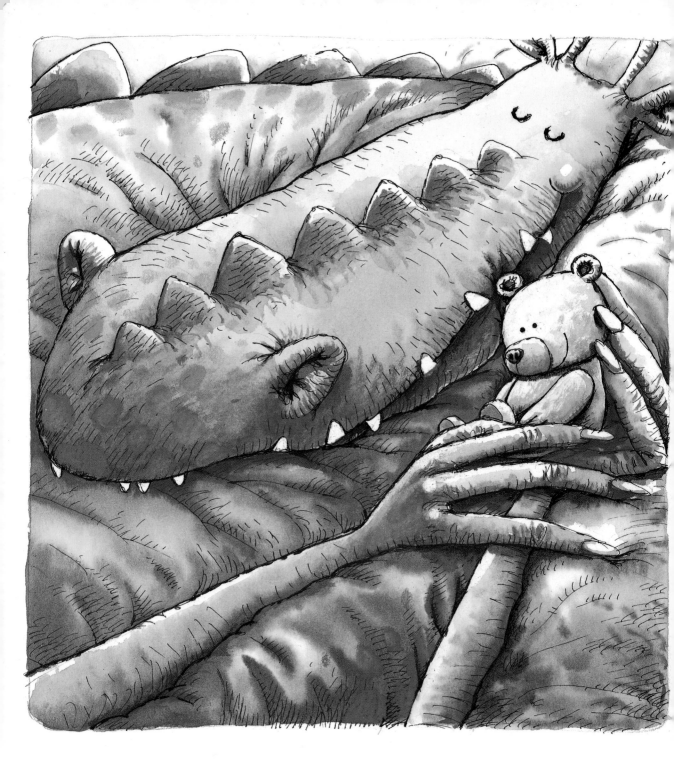

sleep.